Tiptoe Into Scary Cities

SPOOKY NEW ORLEANS

by Kathryn Camisa

Consultant: Debbie Felton
Professor of Classics
University of Massachusetts
Amherst, Massachusetts

BEARPORT PUBLISHING

New York, New York

Credits

Cover, © Colin D. Young/Shutterstock, © DarkBird/Shutterstock, and © Squint Photography/Shutterstock; TOC, © Travelview/Shutterstock; 4–5, © Frontpage/Shutterstock, © Victor Torres/Shutterstock, © David Litman/Shutterstock, © Donna Beeler/Shutterstock, and © Neil Lockhart/Shutterstock; 6, © Nik Merkulov/Shutterstock; 7, © Richard Koch/Library of Congress; 8, © Enzo Cositore/Alamy; 9, © Richard Koch/Library of Congress and © duncan1890/iStock; 10L, © North Wind Picture Archive/Alamy; 10R, Public Domain; 11, © Kathleen K. Parker/Shutterstock; 12, © Vera Petruk/Shutterstock; 13, © Darrell Miller/CC BY-NC 4.0; 14 (L to R), © Africa Studio/Shutterstock and © losmandarinas/Shutterstock;15, © legacy1995/iStock; 16, © alfocome/Shutterstock; 17, © Irene Abdow/Alamy; 18, © ArtMari/Shutterstock; 19, © Images-USA/Alamy; 20, © Sergey Peterman/Shutterstock; 21, © ZUMA Press, Inc./Alamy and © Donna Beeler/Shutterstock; 23, © A Cotton Photo/Shutterstock.

Publisher: Kenn Goin
Senior Editor: Joyce Tavolacci
Creative Director: Spencer Brinker
Photo Researcher: Thomas Persano
Cover: Kim Jones

Library of Congress Cataloging-in-Publication Data

Names: Camisa, Kathryn, author.
Title: Spooky New Orleans / by Kathryn Camisa ; consultant, Debbie Felton, Professor of Classics, University of Massachusetts, Amherst, Massachusetts.
Description: New York : Bearport Publishing Company, Inc., 2019. | Series: Tiptoe into scary cities | Includes bibliographical references and index.
Identifiers: LCCN 2018014148 (print) | LCCN 2018020648 (ebook) | ISBN 9781684027125 (ebook) | ISBN 9781684026661 (library)
Subjects: LCSH: Ghosts—Louisiana—New Orleans—Juvenile literature. | Haunted places—Louisiana—New Orleans—Juvenile literature.
Classification: LCC BF1472.U6 (ebook) | LCC BF1472.U6 C3528 2018 (print) | DDC 133.109763/35—dc23
LC record available at https://lccn.loc.gov/2018014148

For more information, write to Bearport Publishing Company, Inc., 45 West 21st Street, Suite 3B, New York, New York 10010. Printed in the United States of America.

10 9 8 7 6 5 4 3 2 1

CONTENTS

Spooky New Orleans

By day, New Orleans's streets are filled with music and laughter. At night, people whisper about this Louisiana city's spooky side. They tell tales of vampires and ghosts. Watch out—this is a city where the dead still roam.

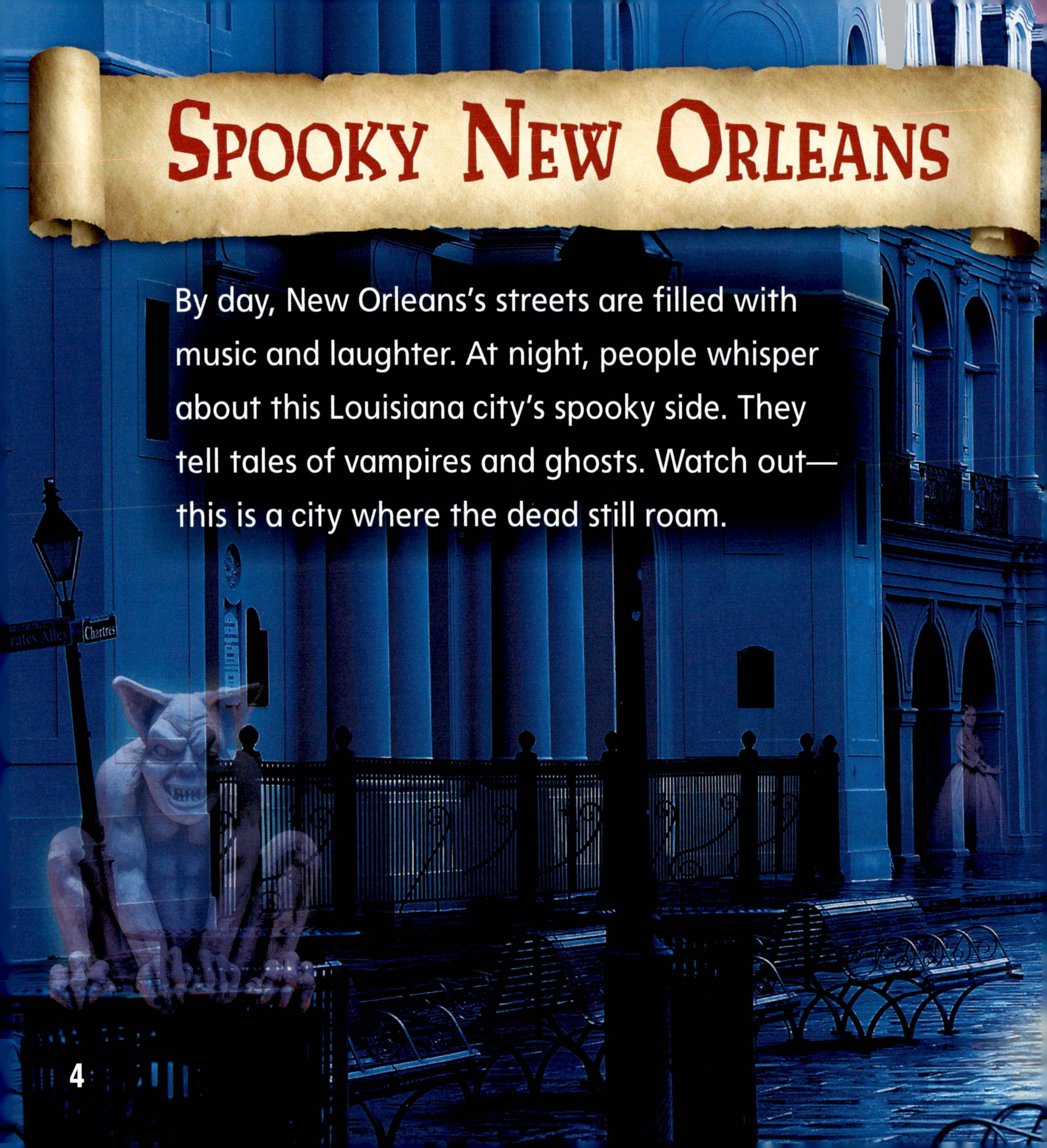

Get ready to read four hair-raising stories about New Orleans. Turn the page . . . if you dare!

Buried Alive

Le Pretre Mansion

It was the late 1800s. A man was strolling down Dauphine Street. As he turned the corner, he saw a trail of blood. It was running down the steps of the Le Pretre **Mansion.** He ran to tell the police.

When the police arrived, they discovered a **gruesome** scene. The home was covered in blood. Outside, a hand stuck out of a freshly dug grave!

Le Pretre Mansion

It's said that the mansion's owner, Prince Suleyman, had thrown a party the night before. The police soon discovered that the dead body was his. And he had been buried alive! Who had killed him? The crime was never solved.

Soon after, neighbors heard party music coming from the empty house. Sometimes, a male figure has been seen there. Is the prince searching for his killer?

The interior of the mansion

"I never feel alone in this building," says a **resident** of the mansion.

Haunted Grounds

St. Roch's Cemetery

The deadly **disease** yellow fever was common in the 1800s. Many thousands of people died from it. During one **outbreak**, Reverend P. L. Thevis prayed to **Saint** Roch to protect the members of his church.

A victim of yellow fever

Saint Roch lived more than 600 years ago. He was known for helping the sick.

Amazingly, none of the church-goers died of yellow fever. In 1874, Thevis built a **shrine** and **cemetery** in the saint's honor.

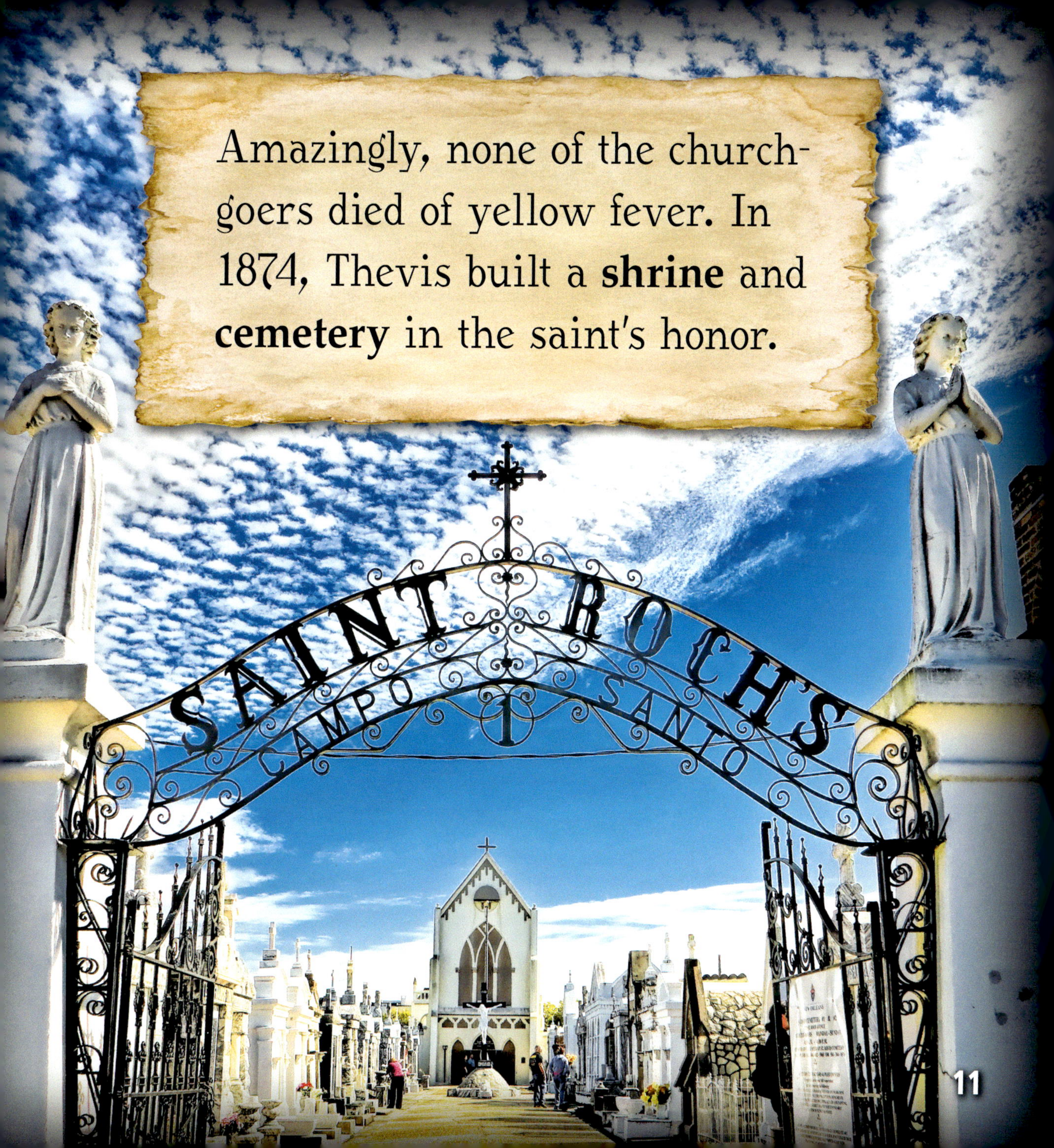

Today, people leave gifts for Saint Roch at the cemetery. They bring flowers, dolls, and notes. All the objects are stored in the shrine.

The cemetery is also said to be the home of a **spirit**. At night, a hooded figure wanders around. The ghost appears to walk through gravestones. Other times, it **vanishes** into thin air!

Gifts left by people at St. Roch's shrine

Restless Spirit

New Orleans Pharmacy Museum

It's after midnight at the museum. An alarm goes off. The police arrive. There's no sign of a break-in, yet the place is in ruins.

The police check the **security** camera. They see a blurry shape in a lab coat. The figure throws books and smashes bottles. Who—or what—is it?

New Orleans Pharmacy Museum

In the 1800s, the museum was a **pharmacy.** The owner, Dr. Joseph Dupas, made his own medicine. However, his customers never seemed to get better. In fact, many died. Some believe Dr. Dupas poisoned them!

In 1867, Dr. Dupas passed away. Is he still making medicine—and trouble—long after his death?

Some visitors experience stomach pain and headaches at the museum. Is it Dr. Dupas at work?

Inside the New Orleans Pharmacy Museum

A Ghostly Vision

Hotel Monteleone

Visitors check out of Hotel Monteleone every day. Unfortunately, one guest never leaves.

In the late 1800s, a young couple was staying at the hotel with their son, Maurice. One night, the boy came down with a high fever. A doctor tried to help him, but Maurice died.

Hotel Monteleone

Each year, Maurice's parents returned to the hotel. They missed their lost son. One night, the boy's ghost appeared to his mother. He told her, "Mommy, don't cry. I'm fine."

Since then, the ghost of a young boy often appears where Maurice died. One guest even woke up to see the boy's ghost at the foot of her bed!

There's a door in the hotel that opens and closes on its own. Is Maurice to blame?

Spooky Spots in New Orleans

Glossary

cemetery (SEM-uh-ter-ee) an area of land where dead bodies are buried

disease (duh-ZEEZ) a sickness or illness

gruesome (GROO-suhm) horrible and disgusting

mansion (MAN-shuhn) a very large, grand house

outbreak (OUT-brake) the sudden spread of a disease

pharmacy (FAR-muh-see) a place where medicine is prepared and sold to people

resident (REZ-uh-duhnt) a person who lives in a particular place

saint (SAYNT) a holy person in the Christian religion

security (si-KYOOR-ih-tee) related to making something safe

shrine (SHRINE) a place that contains special or holy objects

spirit (SPIHR-it) an otherworldly creature, such as a ghost

vanishes (VAN-ish-iz) disappears from sight

Index

Read More

Camisa, Kathryn. *Creepy Schools (Tiptoe Into Scary Places).* New York: Bearport (2018).

Claybourne, Anna. *Don't Read This Book Before Bed: Thrills, Chills, and Hauntingly True Stories.* Washington, DC: National Geographic (2017).

Learn More Online

To learn more about spooky New Orleans, visit:
www.bearportpublishing.com/Tiptoe

About the Author

Kathryn Camisa has visited New Orleans many times. Unfortunately, she's never encountered any ghosts during her trips.